WHERE FOOD COMES FROM

Janet Cook and Shirley Bond S.R.D.

Designed by Chris Scollen
Illustrated by Teri Gower and Guy Smith
Editorial assistance from Felicity Brooks

Contents

2	About food	16	Sugar and chocolate
4	Bread	18	Breakfast cereal
6	Milk and eggs	19	Pasta
8	Cheese and butter	20	Rice
10	Fruit and vegetables	22	Drinks
12	Fish	24	Index
14	Meat		

About food

You need lots of different types of food to keep you strong, fit and healthy. This book explains where each type of food comes from and what happens to it before it reaches your plate.

The story of food

Long ago, people spent most of their time searching for seeds and berries to eat.

They also hunted animals. Often they could not find any food and they had to go hungry.

Famines

Some parts of the world, for example North Africa, have poor soil and hardly any rain. In a very dry year little grows. People have no money to buy food from elsewhere.

North Africa

Sometimes they have to eat seeds which should be planted for the following year. The next year they starve. This is called a famine.

Later they discovered how to tame animals. They protected them from wolves, then killed them when they needed food.

After a while, they found out how to grow plants by sprinkling seeds on the ground. They then ate these plants.

They now had all their food around them in one place. Because of this, people were much less likely to go hungry.

Swapping food

Some food can only grow in a particular climate. For example, grapes need plenty of warm sun, and rice needs lots of rain.

Many kinds of food are sent abroad. This means people in cool places can buy grapes and people in dry places can buy rice.

Goods going into a country are called imports. Goods sent out of a country are called exports.

Rain dances

American Indians used to believe that rain was sent by rain gods. They tried to please these gods by dancing for them. They hoped this would make the gods send rain to help their crops grow.

Preserving food

Fresh food can soon go bad. Because of this, food is treated so it lasts longer and is safe to eat.

Freezing
Frozen food will keep for many months in a freezer.

Pickling
Some foods are put in jars of vinegar.

Canning
Food is put into clean tins which are sealed and heated.

Drying
Some foods, such as fruit and wheat, can be dried in the sun.

Pickled eggs

Frozen peas

Frozen fish

Dried apple rings

Pickled onions

Oats

Baked beans

Tomatoes

Dried figs

Wheat

3

Bread

Have you noticed how many different sorts of bread there are? Here are just a few of them.

Bread is made mostly of flour. The colour and taste depends on what type of flour the baker uses.

What is flour?

Most flour comes from a type of grass known as wheat*. The seeds or grains are removed and crushed to make flour.

Wheat

Grain

Split loaf
Chollah
Cottage loaf
Bloomer
Pitta bread
Sandwich loaf
Soda bread
Rolls
Chapatti
Baps
Naan bread
Rye bread

French stick

What happens at the bakery?

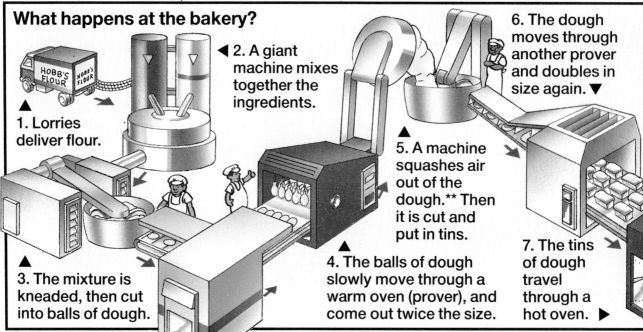

1. Lorries deliver flour.

2. A giant machine mixes together the ingredients.

3. The mixture is kneaded, then cut into balls of dough.

4. The balls of dough slowly move through a warm oven (prover), and come out twice the size.

5. A machine squashes air out of the dough.** Then it is cut and put in tins.

6. The dough moves through another prover and doubles in size again. ▼

7. The tins of dough travel through a hot oven. ▶

HOBB'S FLOUR

*Rye bread is made from a different sort of grass called rye.
**This is called knocking back.

Make your own bread

Home-made bread tastes delicious.

You will need:

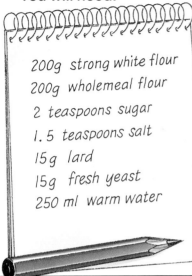

200g strong white flour
200g wholemeal flour
2 teaspoons sugar
1.5 teaspoons salt
15g lard
15g fresh yeast
250 ml warm water

1. Mix the yeast and water. Now mix everything to make dough.

2. Fold the dough towards you then push it down and away.

Loaf tin

3. Turn it and repeat until it's no longer sticky. Put it in a tin.

4. Rub oil in a plastic bag. Put the tin in it. Leave in a warm place.

5. After an hour, remove from the bag and bake in a hot oven* for half an hour.

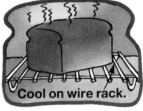

Cool on wire rack.

6. Remove from the tin. Does it sound hollow when tapped underneath?**

10. The bread ▶ is delivered to the shops.

9. Some are sliced and wrapped.

8. The loaves are tipped out of their tins and cooled on racks.

What makes bread rise?

If you make your own bread, you will see that the finished loaf is bigger than the dough you started with. The ingredient which makes dough grow (rise) is the yeast.

When it is warm, yeast gives off tiny bubbles of a gas called carbon dioxide. It is the bubbles that makes the dough rise.

Look at a slice of bread. Can you see tiny holes left by the carbon dioxide?

Flat bread

Some bread is made without yeast, and is quite flat. This is unleavened bread. There are four types shown on the opposite page; can you guess which ones? (Answer on page 24.)

*Gas mark 8, or 450°F, 230°C (electric).
**If it doesn't, put it back in the tin and leave for about five minutes longer.

Milk and eggs

Most milk comes from cows. A cow cannot give us milk until she has had her first calf. After that, she produces much more than a calf could drink; about 4,000 litres each year.

At the farm

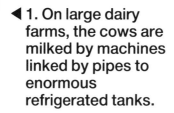

◀ 1. On large dairy farms, the cows are milked by machines linked by pipes to enormous refrigerated tanks.

2. Each day, a refrigerated tanker collects the milk and takes it to the dairy. ▼

Tank

The milk flows from the tank to the lorry through this pipe.

How cream is made

Warm milk is poured into a centrifuge. This machine separates the cream by spinning the milk very quickly.

A switch on the centrifuge controls how thick the cream is.

Very thin – single

Thin – whipping

Thick – double

Very thick – clotted

You can tell how thick cream is by its name.

JOE'S DAIRY

The dairy has to be very clean and hygienic.

Tankers with milk from lots of farms in the area.

At the dairy

3. The milk is tested to make sure it is clean. Most milk is then heated for around 15 seconds, then quickly cooled down.

This is called pasteurising. It destroys any harmful germs in the milk and keeps it fresh for longer.

4. Machines pour the milk into cartons, bottles or cans. They are then loaded on to lorries and delivered to shops.

6

Make your own yoghurt

You will need:

750 ml longlife milk

2 teaspoons fresh
natural yoghurt

2-3 tablespoons
dried skimmed milk

chopped fruit or
nuts (optional)

1. Mix a little longlife milk and the yoghurt.

2. Stir in the remaining milk and the dried milk.

3. Cover with a tea-towel, and leave in a warm place.

4. After about 12 hours, add chopped fruit or nuts.

Crate of milk bottles

Milk lorry

Eggs

Most of the eggs you eat come from chickens. Sometimes the egg box tells you about the lives of the chickens that laid them.

★ Free range chickens roam around a farmyard, eating whatever they find. You have to hunt for the eggs.

★ Deep litter chickens live in a warm shed with straw on the floor. The farmer gives them special food.

★ Battery chickens are kept in cages and given special food. The eggs are collected from a tray below the cage.

From the farm to the box

Every day, large farms send eggs to a packing station. Here, workers measure them, then shine a bright light on them which shows if any are bad. They then pack them into boxes.

How fresh is your egg?

Place your egg in a glass bowl full of water. Now watch to see what it does.

Fresh	Not so fresh	Bad

There is an airspace inside one end of the egg. The older the egg, the larger the space, and the more likely it is to float.

Cheese and butter

Butter and cheese are both made from milk. Here you can find out how they are made. You can also discover why margarine was first invented.

The story of butter

▲ Long ago, a traveller took some milk for his journey. He hung it in a leather bag around his camel's neck. It jerked around, and when he came to drink it, it had turned almost solid. This was butter.

Almost 200 ▶ years ago, people put cream in a tub with a pole in the middle (a butter churn). To make butter, they pulled the pole up and down.

Today, a machine can produce almost three tonnes of butter an hour.

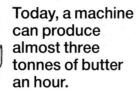

Cheese

There are lots of types of cheeses made all over the world. Many are named after the place where they were first made.

Most are now made in factories, and sold all round the world.

How is cheese made?

Every cheese is made differently. Here you can see how five sorts are made. If you want to find out about cheddar (letter B), for example, follow the writing with B above it.

KEY

A	Gruyère	
B	Cheddar	
C	Brie	
D	Stilton	
E	Cottage cheese	

START

ABCD
1. Fresh milk is pasteurised.

E
1. Skimmed milk is pasteurised.

ABCDE
2. The milk is put into cheese vats.

ABCD
4. The milk is warmed, then rennet is added. This turns it lumpy.

ABDE
3. Bacteria is added. This makes the milk sour.

Margarine

About 150 years ago, there was a shortage of butter in France. Hipolyte Mège Mouriès invented margarine. It looked like butter but had a pearly shine.

The word margarine comes from the Greek margaritarion, meaning pearl.

Nowadays, most margarine is made from vegetable oil which is pumped with gas to make it go solid. Extra ingredients are then added to make it look like butter.

A

6. The lumps are cooked, pressed in moulds, then left in a cellar for six months. Here the cheese gives off bubbles. This makes holes in it.

B

6. The lumps are wrapped in cloth and pressed in moulds.

Brie has to be made flat so that the inside ripens quite quickly.

C

6. The lumps are left until the surface goes mouldy. This ripens the cheese from the outside inwards.

D

5. The liquid is drained away very slowly to leave moist lumps.

C

5. The milk is cut, so some of the liquid drains away.

ABE

5. The milk is cut, so the liquid drains away.

D

6. The lumps are left in ripening rooms. Here they are pierced with needles. This lets air in and makes it mouldy.

E

6. The lumps are washed, drained, and divided into small pieces.

FINISH

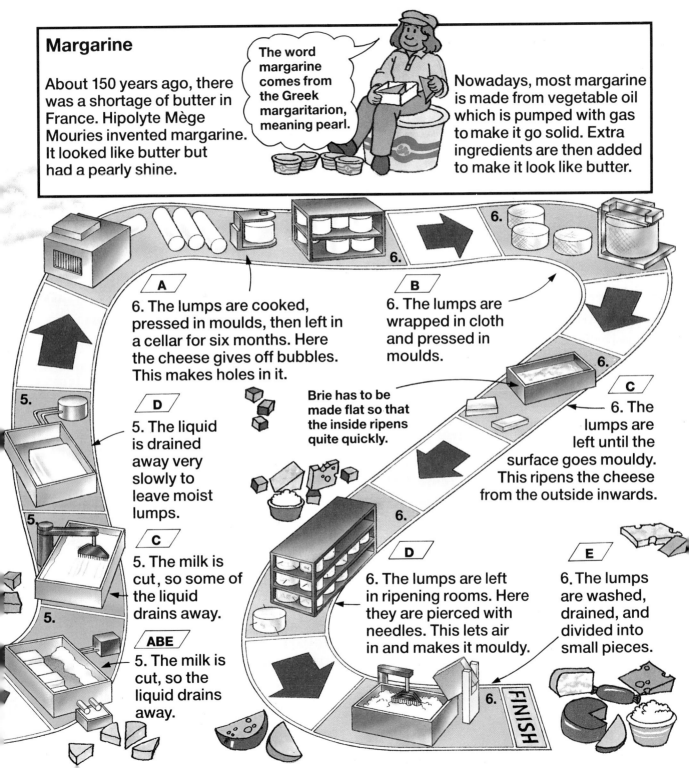

Fruit and vegetables

Some fruit and vegetables are grown in this country, but many are bought from countries which have a different climate.

They are all plants or parts of plants such as roots and stems.

You eat the centre of an artichoke, and the bottom of its petals.

Celery

Asparagus

These are the bulbs of plants.

These are the leaves of plants, picked before the flower comes out.

Onion

Leek

These are the stems of plants.

Spring onion

Lettuce
Endive
Spinach
Cabbage

Broccoli

Nuts

Most nuts are fruits or seeds that come from trees. Coconuts come from a type of palm tree.

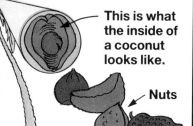

This is what the inside of a coconut looks like.

Nuts

These vegetables are the flowers of plants.

Cauliflower

These are the roots or underground stems (tubers) of plants.

Potato

Tomato

Courgette

Carrot

These vegetables are the fruits of plants.

Pulses

Dried beans, peas and lentils are called pulses. They must be soaked before being cooked.

Chick peas

Haricot beans

Red kidney beans

Chilli

Cucumber

Pepper

Sweetcorn is made into cornflakes, popcorn and a type of flour (cornflour).

How bananas get here

Banana tree

Bananas grow in hot places like the West Indies. A large red flower comes out of the middle of the trunk. When this opens up there is a stem with about 100 bananas on it.

See page 3 for more about importing.

Apple

Orange

Lemon

Grapefruit

Grapes grow on a plant called a vine. Some are dried to make raisins. Some are made into wine.

These are called citrus fruits. They grow on trees.

Apples and pears can be eaten raw, but some are better cooked.

Berries and soft fruit grow on bushes or plants.

Strawberry **Mango**

Most mushrooms are grown especially for eating. Wild ones can look like poisonous toadstools, so don't pick them.

Avocado
Peach

Cherry

Dates grow on palm trees.

These are stone fruit (they have a stone in the middle). They grow on trees.

Plum

Making crisps

Crisps are made from potatoes.

First the potatoes are washed and peeled.

A machine ▶ slices them thinly. They are fried in hot oil, then drained and sprinkled with salt and flavourings.

◀ A machine weighs the crisps into bags.

◀ The stems are unloaded and taken to warm, damp rooms. When they are nearly ripe, they are cut into bunches called hands.

These are sent to fruit markets and shops all over ▼ the country.

▲ The bananas are picked when they are still hard and green.

▲ On board ship, they are kept cool so they don't ripen too quickly.

TROPICO

Fish

Most fish are caught at sea in nets dangling from boats called fishing trawlers. The fish have to be rushed back to port very quickly, before they go bad.

Sometimes the fish are stored in freezers on the trawler instead.

Deep sea trawler

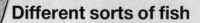

Open purse seine net

Catching fish

Deep sea trawlers catch fish from the bottom of the sea. They drag their nets along the sea-bed.

A trawler with a purse seine net catches fish which swim nearer the surface. Once the net is full, fishermen pull in the rope around the top of it.

The life of a salmon

When a salmon is about two years old it swims downstream towards the ocean.

After four years in the sea, it returns to its original river, using the sun to find its way. It knows its home by its smell.

The salmon leaps over anything in its path.

Most salmon then stay in the river until they die, but a few do the journey again.

Different sorts of fish

There are more than 30,000 different sorts of fish living in the seas, rivers, streams, lakes and ponds around the world. There are four main groups of fish: white fish, oily fish, freshwater fish and shellfish.

Oily fish, ▶ such as mackerel, mostly live in the sea.

Mackerel

White fish can ▶ be round (such as haddock), or flat (such as plaice).

Plaice

◀ Freshwater fish, such as trout and salmon, mostly live in lakes and rivers.

Trout

Crabs ◀ Shellfish (such as crabs, prawns and mussels) mostly live on the sea-bed.

Mussels

Prawns

Preserving fish

Unless fish is eaten very soon after it is caught, it has to be treated to stop it from going bad. You can get food poisoning from bad fish.

Drying ▶
Long ago, people learnt to dry fish in the sun and wind.

Smoking ▶
Hanging fish over a fire preserves it and gives it a smokey flavour.

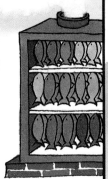

Freezing ▶
Fish lasts for up to three months in the freezer.

Salting ▶
Ancient Egyptians used salt to preserve fish.

Pickling ▶
Soaking fish in vinegar and salt is known as pickling.

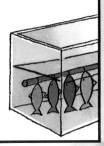

How fish fingers are made

1. The parts that make fish fingers are removed and washed.

5. They are ▶ sprinkled with breadcrumbs.

6. The fingers are then quickly fried to make the coating go hard.

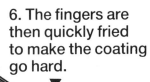

Frozen fish

2. They are frozen in large blocks.

3. Machines cut the blocks into fingers.

4. These go through a mixture of flour, starch, water and salt.

7. They are refrozen and packed. ▶

8. They are ▶ taken to shops in refrigerated lorries.

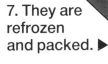

Meat

People have always killed animals for food. Cavemen spent their days hunting animals, and in some places there are still tribes of people who hunt animals.

Most of the meat we eat nowadays comes from farm animals.

Red and white meat

There are two main types of meat; red meat and white meat. Beef, lamb and pork are all red meat.

White meat comes from birds such as chickens, turkeys and ducks.

◀ Beef comes from cows. Most cows are killed when they are between the age of one and two. Meat from a young calf is called veal.

Chicken

Duck

Turkey

Pork and bacon both ▲ come from pigs. Pigs are killed when they are the right weight.

Lambs are usually killed ▲ when they are a year old. After this, the meat is called hoggett or mutton.

From the farmer to your plate

Here you can see what happens to the animals before they get to your plate.

Farmer

Cows and sheep mainly eat grass. In the winter, other crops such as hay and barley are also given to them.

Pigs like lots of different foods. Famers give them a special mixture called pig swill.

Auction market

Live animals are taken to market by the farmer. Cattle are sold one by one. Pigs and sheep are weighed and sold in groups.

Abattoir

The animals are killed, then stored until they are sold.

Most meat is sold direct to butchers. Some is taken to meat markets.

Cooking meat

Meat has to be cooked before we eat it, to destroy any germs in it and make it tender and tasty.

Roasting is a way of cooking the large pieces (joints) in the ▶ oven.

▲
Stewing is the best way to cook meat which is not very tender. The meat is cooked in liquid inside, or on top of, the cooker.

◀ Grilling is a good way of cooking small, tender pieces of meat such as chops.

▲
Frying is cooking meat in fat in a shallow pan.

▲
Stir-frying is similar to normal frying. You toss thin strips of meat in a wok.

▲
Barbecuing is when meat is cooked on a barbecue outside.

▲
Braising means frying meat quickly, then adding liquid. The pot is then covered and put in the oven or left on top of the cooker.

Meat markets
These sell meat to butchers. One famous market is Smithfield in London. Butchers often buy a whole body. This is called a carcass.

Butcher
The butcher cuts the carcass up to sell it. Other things such as sausages and beefburgers are also made out of the meat.

Non meat-eaters
Some people, called vegetarians, don't eat meat or fish. They may think it is wrong to kill, or dislike the way some animals are kept. Some have religious reasons. For example, Hindus don't eat beef, and Jews won't eat pork.

Vegetarians eat lots of fruit and vegetables.

Sugar and chocolate

Sugar and chocolate both come from plants. Below you can find out what happens to the plants after they are picked.

Sugar

Sugar comes from sugar cane or sugar beet plants. Below you can see what is done to the plants to make brown sugar.

Sugar cane

Sugar from cane and sugar from beet look and taste the same.

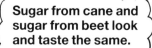

The juice inside the thick stalks contains all the sugar.

▲
1. The tall canes are cut down and taken to a factory called a sugar mill.

2. They are shredded and crushed between rollers that squeeze out the juice. ▲

Lime
▲
3. The juice is boiled with lime. This gets rid of the unwanted bits in the juice. It is then boiled to make syrup and small lumps of sugar (crystals).

Sugar beet
Sugar beet plants look a bit like parsnips. They grow in cool places.

1. The leaves ▶ are removed, and the plants are taken to a factory.

◀ 2. Here they are washed, sliced and spun in hot water.

3. The sugar passes out into the water. This is boiled, then treated like ◀ cane juice.

4. A centrifuge* separates the brown crystals from the syrup.
▼

5. The crystals are taken to other countries to be made into white sugar. ▼

*You can find out about centrifuges on page 6.

Making white sugar

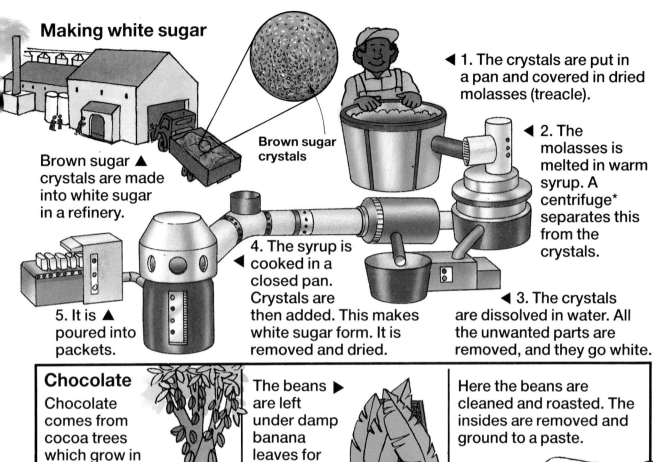

Brown sugar ▲ crystals are made into white sugar in a refinery.

Brown sugar crystals

◄ 1. The crystals are put in a pan and covered in dried molasses (treacle).

◄ 2. The molasses is melted in warm syrup. A centrifuge* separates this from the crystals.

◄ 3. The crystals are dissolved in water. All the unwanted parts are removed, and they go white.

4. The syrup is ◄ cooked in a closed pan. Crystals are then added. This makes white sugar form. It is removed and dried.

5. It is ▲ poured into packets.

Chocolate

Chocolate comes from cocoa trees which grow in South America and Africa.

Cocoa beans ► grow in large pods which are picked when they are ripe.

Pod

Bean

Each pod contains about 40 beans.

The beans ► are left under damp banana leaves for six days, to give them a nice taste.

They are dried in the sun, put in sacks and shipped to factories abroad. ▼

Here the beans are cleaned and roasted. The insides are removed and ground to a paste.

Cocoa ► butter is squeezed out of the paste.

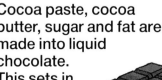

Cocoa paste, cocoa butter, sugar and fat are made into liquid chocolate. This sets in moulds. ►

17

Breakfast cereal

Most breakfast cereals are made from crops which grow in fields. For example, muesli is made from oats. Below you can see how cornflakes are made.

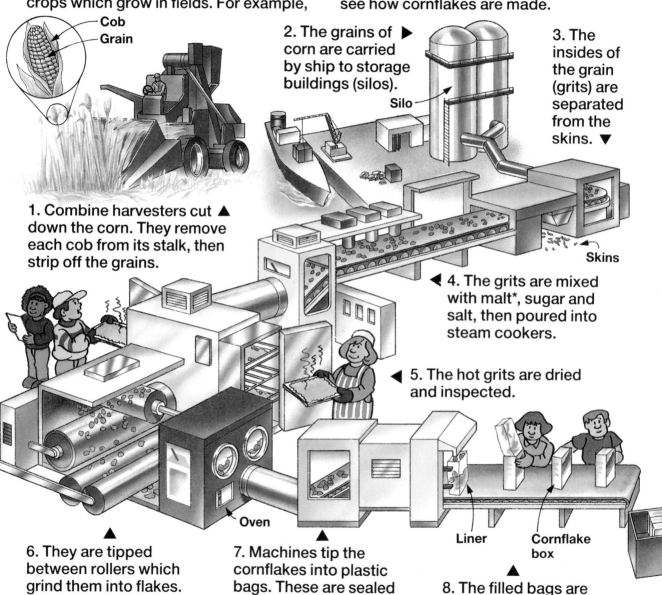

Cob
Grain

2. The grains of ▶ corn are carried by ship to storage buildings (silos).

Silo

3. The insides of the grain (grits) are separated from the skins. ▼

Skins

1. Combine harvesters cut ▲ down the corn. They remove each cob from its stalk, then strip off the grains.

4. The grits are mixed with malt*, sugar and salt, then poured into steam cookers. ◀

5. The hot grits are dried and inspected. ◀

Oven

Liner

Cornflake box

6. They are tipped between rollers which grind them into flakes. Then they are toasted in turning ovens. ▲

7. Machines tip the cornflakes into plastic bags. These are sealed to stop any air making the cornflakes go soft. ▲

8. The filled bags are put in boxes. These are then delivered to shops. ▲

*Malt is barley that has sprouted and then been dried.

Pasta

Pasta is made out of semolina. This is wheat (see page 4) which has been rolled and sieved into even grains.

Below you can see how spaghetti is made.

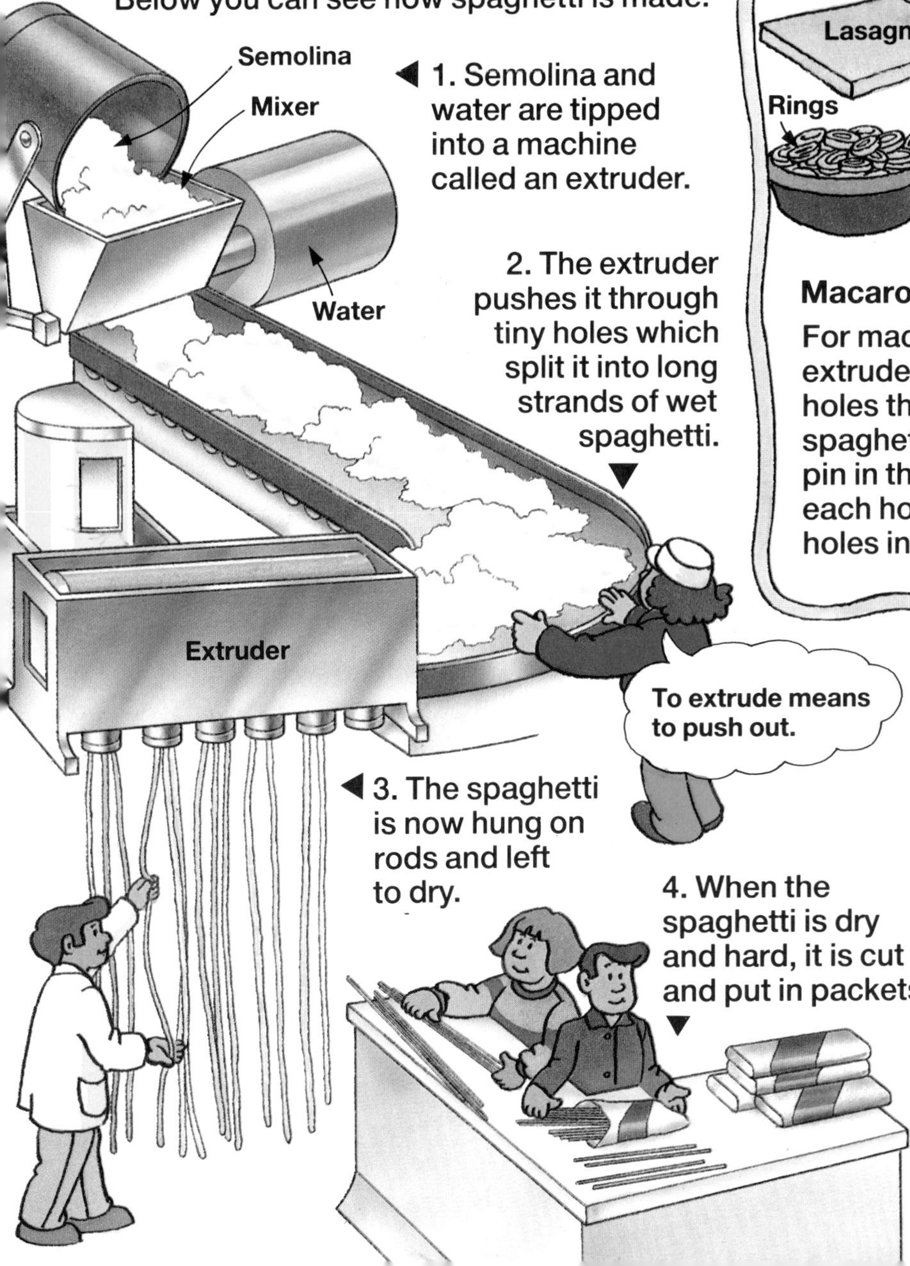

Semolina

Mixer

Water

1. Semolina and water are tipped into a machine called an extruder.

2. The extruder pushes it through tiny holes which split it into long strands of wet spaghetti.

Extruder

To extrude means to push out.

3. The spaghetti is now hung on rods and left to dry.

4. When the spaghetti is dry and hard, it is cut and put in packets.

Other sorts of pasta

The extruder can make pasta in all sorts of shapes and sizes. A few are shown here.

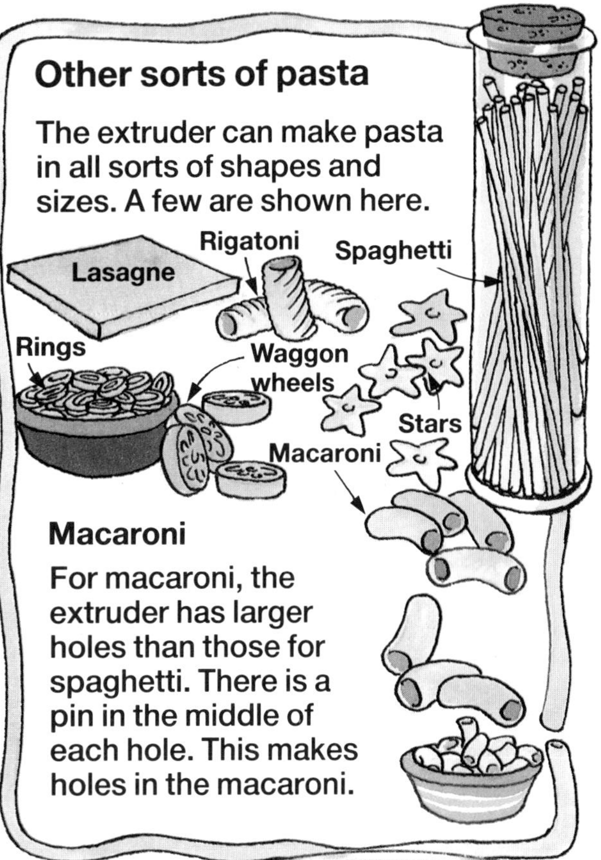

Lasagne

Rigatoni

Spaghetti

Rings

Waggon wheels

Stars

Macaroni

Macaroni

For macaroni, the extruder has larger holes than those for spaghetti. There is a pin in the middle of each hole. This makes holes in the macaroni.

Tinned spaghetti

Some spaghetti is sent to factories. Here it is cooked, chopped up and put into cans with tomato sauce.

19

Rice

90% of the world's rice is grown and eaten in China and the East. The rest comes from the USA. In the USA, modern machines are used. These make rice-growing quick and efficient. In China and the East, rice is still grown by hand, as shown below.

1. Sacks of seeds (paddy) are put in water. They are left to sprout.

2. Sprouts are sown in a sheltered area, and looked after for a month. ▼

3. A large field is now flooded. Oxen are used to dig trenches. ▼

4. Workers place the small plants in trenches. ▼

5. When the plants are bigger, workers turn water wheels with their feet. This lets more water in.

6. Each plant is sprayed to stop rats, birds and insects eating them.

7. The fields are drained. The workers then cut down the rice with scythes (large knives).

8. The rice is tied and left to dry for a few days.

9. The rice is threshed (beaten) to separate grains from the stalks.

10. The grains are sieved and winnowed (tossed) to remove all the dirt. They are then put in sacks.

The first American rice

In 1694, a ship carrying rice and spices was sailing from Madagascar. A storm blew up, and the ship had to shelter in Charleston, USA.

The captain gave the people some sacks of rice seed. They planted this seed, and soon there was enough rice for everyone in South Carolina.

Different sorts of rice

There are three main sorts of rice:

★ Long grain rice is good with savoury dishes such as curry.
★ Medium grain rice is used for both savoury and sweet dishes.
★ Short grain rice is good for rice puddings.

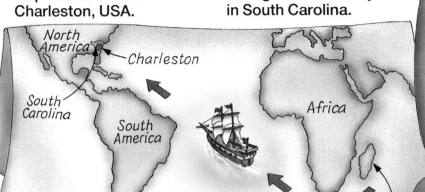

Long grain rice

Medium grain rice

Short grain rice

Make your own rice pudding

This recipe makes a thick, creamy pudding with a sugary skin on top. You will need:

100g short grain rice

850ml milk

75g sugar

2 eggs (optional)

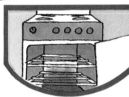

1. Heat the oven to Gas Mark 2.*

2. Heat the rice and milk in a saucepan.

3. Let the rice simmer for 10 minutes.

4. Let the rice cool. Beat the eggs in a bowl.

5. Mix everything together and put in a dish.

Baking dish

6. Bake in the oven for about half an hour.

*Electric ovens: 150°C or 300°F.

Drinks

Below you can find out how fizzy drinks are made.

You can also see where coffee and tea come from.

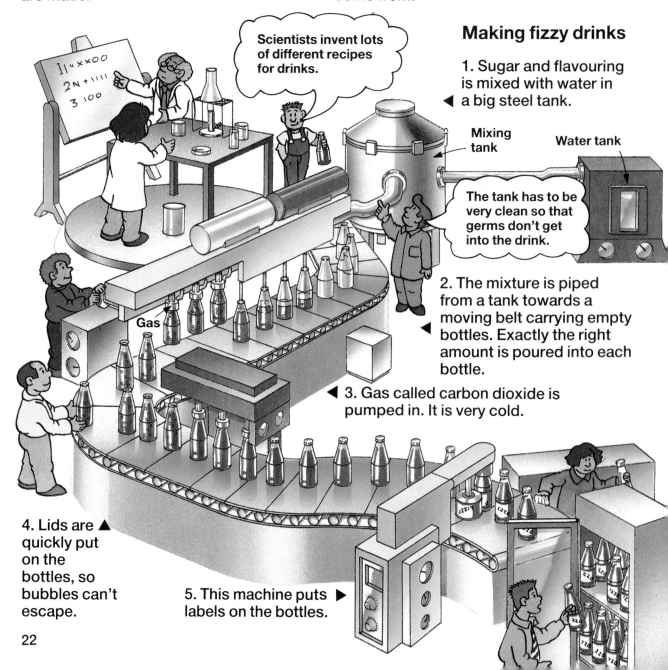

Scientists invent lots of different recipes for drinks.

Making fizzy drinks

1. Sugar and flavouring is mixed with water in a big steel tank.

Mixing tank

Water tank

The tank has to be very clean so that germs don't get into the drink.

2. The mixture is piped from a tank towards a moving belt carrying empty bottles. Exactly the right amount is poured into each bottle.

3. Gas called carbon dioxide is pumped in. It is very cold.

Gas

4. Lids are quickly put on the bottles, so bubbles can't escape.

5. This machine puts labels on the bottles.

The life of a coffee bean

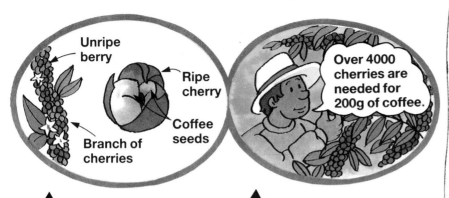

Unripe berry

Ripe cherry

Coffee seeds

Branch of cherries

Over 4000 cherries are needed for 200g of coffee.

▲
1. Berries from coffee trees are dark green at first. As they ripen they go yellow, then they turn deep red and are called cherries.

▲
2. The cherries are picked or left until they fall off the trees. They are then collected and sifted to remove the dust, leaves and twigs.

Pulper

60kg sacks

▲
3. A machine removes the flesh (pulp). The outsides are washed, dried and put in a machine called a huller. The parts that are left are called beans.

▲
4. Sacks of beans are shipped abroad.
The beans are roasted. Some are sold whole. Others are ground into granules or powder.

Where does coffee grow?

Coffee trees need plenty of warm weather. If it is too hot or cold, they will die.

TROPIC OF CANCER

North America

Europe

Africa

South America

Australia

TROPIC OF CAPRICORN

Most coffee is grown between the Tropic of Cancer and the Tropic of Capricorn.

Tea

Tea leaves grow on bushes mainly in China and India.
Before modern ships were built, tea was carried to many countries in ships called clippers.

Tea clipper

23

Index

abattoir, 14

bacteria, 8
banana, 10-11
    leaves, 17
beef, 14,15
bread, 4-5
breakfast cereal, 18
butter, 8

carbon dioxide, 5,22
carcasses, 14
centrifuge, 16,17
cheese, 8-9
chemicals, 20
chocolate, 17
cobs, 18
cocoa, 17
coconuts, 10
coffee, 23
cooking meat, 15
cornflakes, 18
cows, 6,14
cream, 6,8,
crisps, 11
crops, 14,18
curds, 9

dough, 5
drinks, 22-23

eggs, 7
exports, 3,8

famines, 2
farms, 6, 7, 14

fish, 12-13
    fingers, 13
fishing, 12
flour, 4
food poisoning, 13
fruit, 10-11

germs, 6,15,22
grains, 4,18,19,20

Hindus, 15
Hipolyte Mège Mouries, 9
hoggett, 14
huller, 23

imports, 3,8,10

lamb, 14

Jews, 15

macaroni, 19
margarine, 9
meat, 14-15
milk, 6-7
molasses, 17
muesli, 18
mutton, 14

nuts,10

paddy, 20
pasta, 19
pork, 14,15
preserving food, 3, 13
pulper, 23

pulses, 10

rain dances, 3
recipe,
    for bread, 4
    for drinks, 22
    for rice pudding, 21
    for yoghurt, 7
rice, 3, 20-21
rye, 4

salmon, 12
semolina, 19
silos, 18
spaghetti, 19
sugar, 16-17

tea, 23

veal, 14
vegetables, 10-11,15
vegetarians, 15

wheat, 4
whey, 9

yeast, 4,5
yoghurt, 7

Answer to page 5

Naan bread, chapattis, soda bread and pitta bread are all unleavened.

First published in 1989 by Usborne Publishing Ltd, 20 Garrick Street, London WC2E 9BJ, England.

Printed in Belgium.